For Bonnie and Abigail and Lily
&
For Vicky and Willie
&
For Whales Everywhere
T.C. & J.F.

In loving memory of
Beverly Barrett Stratton
With love,
J. S.

Sing a Whale Song

Story and Songs by
TOM CHAPIN & JOHN FORSTER

Illustrations by JERRY SMATH

Random House 🏠 New York

All rights reserved under International and Pan-American Copyright Conventions. Published in the United States by Random House, Inc., New York, and simultaneously in Canada by Random House of Canada Limited, Toronto. Distributed by Random House, Inc., New York. Manufactured in the United States of America.

"Sing a Whale Song" by John Forster & Tom Chapin © 1989 Limousine Music Co. & The Last Music Co. (ASCAP). From the Sony Kids' Music release *Moonboat**. Humpback whale songs courtesy of Roger Payne and the Longterm Research Institute.
"Good Garbage" by John Forster & Tom Chapin © 1990 Limousine Music Co. & The Last Music Co. (ASCAP). From the recording *Mother Earth* © 1990 Sundance Music, Inc. Distributed by A & M Records, Inc.
"Someone's Gonna Use It" by John Forster & Tom Chapin © 1988 Limousine Music Co. & The Last Music Co. (ASCAP). From the Sony Kids' Music release *Family Tree**.
"This Pretty Planet" by John Forster & Tom Chapin © 1988 Limousine Music Co. & The Last Music Co. (ASCAP). From the Sony Kids' Music release *Family Tree**. Guest vocals by Judy Collins.

*℗ 1992 Sony Music Entertainment, Inc./Sony Kids' Music

More than anything else, Timothy Finney loved the sea.

Every day after school, he would run down to the dock, where he'd play or fish or just sit, staring into the lapping blue waves, wondering what was over the edge of the world.

"I wish I were out there," Timothy would whisper. "Out on the sea. Maybe a pirate ship could appear and lead me to a golden treasure. Or a magic sea gull could scoop me up and fly me over the seven seas. Or maybe…just maybe…I could become a giant whale and swim down to the deep, where the fishes sleep."

One day Timothy was sitting staring out to sea, when he heard a strange singing sound. The sound grew and suddenly he saw an enormous wave beneath his feet.

He looked down, and there, under his toes, was the face of a great humpback whale.

Timothy held his breath.

"Make a wish," said the whale.

"What can I wish for?" asked Timothy.

"Anything," the whale replied. "Wish for a pirate ship to lead you to a golden treasure. Or for a magic sea gull to fly you over the seven seas. Or—"

"—to become a giant whale!" Timothy cried. "That's my wish!"

The great whale lifted his body out of the water. "Touch my flipper, Timothy," he whispered.

Timothy reached out and touched the smooth, soft skin of the whale. Suddenly, he felt something strange and wonderful happening. He slipped over the side of the dock and into the water, flipping his large gray tail.

His wish had been granted. He had been turned into a beautiful humpback whale! Timothy dove down deep. Then, with a burst of joy, he raced to the surface and flung his body out of the water in a great whale leap.

As he dove again, he heard the other whale speak. "Follow me."

Timothy followed his new friend past reefs of coral and wrecks of ancient wooden ships. The light from above was silvery and pale. In all his days of dreaming and wishing, Timothy had never imagined the ocean would be this beautiful.

His powerful body cut through the water with ease. It was like swimming through silk and velvet.

Timothy and the great whale played tag among the schools of fish. Then they played follow the leader. The whale jumped high, flashing his tail and spouting long streams. When it was Timothy's turn, he tried to jump even higher. The sun warmed his back, and his own spray cooled him again.

Timothy and the great whale swam through warm tropical seas and under the cold polar icecap. Timothy saw fish with golden scales and others that glowed in the dark depths, an underwater rainbow. He saw silly sea horses that made him laugh and long eels that wove themselves through the sea grasses. And when he rose to the surface to breathe, he saw the light of the sun dancing on the water.

"Wow!" Timothy exclaimed. "This must be the prettiest place on Earth!"

"Yes, but it isn't all like this," said the great whale. "Come with me, Timothy. I'll show you."

Timothy and the great whale swam on. Soon they found themselves in another part of the ocean. The silvery light from above had disappeared.

Timothy looked up. The shadow of a garbage scow loomed above him. All around it floated empty bottles and plastic bags.

The great whale shook his head sadly and swam off. Timothy followed.

Later, when Timothy rose to the surface to breathe, he found himself covered with black slime. A huge oil slick coated the water in every direction! Timothy raced off as fast as he could, trying to wash the thick black oil off his skin as he sped through the water. Suddenly, he felt something grab at him. He struggled to break free, but a giant, terrible net held him in its grasp!

"Help me!" cried Timothy. The great whale, who was wise to nets, tore a hole in it and set Timothy free.

"But it was so beautiful before," Timothy said, confused and frightened. "What happened? Why are the oceans full of garbage and oil and giant nets? Is there anything we can do?"

"Perhaps." The voice of the great whale floated up to Timothy. "Follow me."

The whale led Timothy to a small opening in a rocky ledge. When they swam through it, Timothy's eyes grew wide.

They had entered a glorious undersea cavern. Gathered there were members of every family that lived in the ocean.

"Garbage," an oyster was muttering. "They are dumping garbage and sludge into the harbors. It drifts down on us day after day."

"We have to do something," a flounder said. "Humans are throwing their waste into the ocean and poisoning life for all of us."

"But what can we do?" barked a dogfish.

"We must tell people to stop polluting our homes," a great white shark suggested. "After all, the Earth is their home, too."

"But who will carry our message to the people?" wondered the dolphin.

"He will," said the great whale, flipping his tail toward Timothy. "He will sing them my song, the song of our love for the sea. Perhaps then people will understand."

"But I do not know your song," said Timothy.

"I will teach it to you," said the whale.

And the whale began to sing. He sang the most beautiful song Timothy had ever heard. He sang of his brothers and sisters, who wanted to live in harmony with the creatures of the land. He sang to save the homes of whales and fish, sea horses and snails, animals and people.

And Timothy learned the whale's song.

"Now it is time for you to go home," the great whale said to Timothy, "so you can sing my song to all the people of the world."

With a sweep of his tail, the whale lifted Timothy back up onto the dock. And in that moment, Timothy blinked and became a boy again.

That night, snug in his bed, Timothy sang the whale's song over and over to himself so he would not forget it. And as soon as he got up the next morning, he began to sing it to everyone he met.

People heard the song and liked it and began to sing it themselves. A song of how wonderful the Earth had been and could be again. A song of hope for the planet. A whale song.

Sing a Whale Song

On a fateful day in the month of May
I was sitting catching fish,
When a magic whale swam up to the rail
And said, "Please make a wish."
So I said, "Well, gee, I'd love to be like you, a giant whale."
Next thing I knew, I was grayish blue, and I had a two-ton tail.
Sing a whale song.
Sing a whale song.
Sing a whale song.
As the flounder said to the oyster bed, "Sing a whale song!"

With a mighty leap I dove down deep
And swam out through the cove.
Then I raced to the top, did a belly flop, and down again I dove.
From the Arctic to the Baltic to the far-off Hebrides,
Like a submarine through the deep blue-green,
I swam the seven seas and sang a whale song.
Sing a whale song.
Sing a whale song.
As the dogfish barked to the great white shark, "Sing a whale song!"

But there were some things I wish I could forget,
Like that garbage scow off of Curaçao,
Or that oil spill below Brazil,
Or getting caught in that giant net,
And I couldn't get out, and oh, was I upset!

So I had to hail that magic whale, who changed me back once more,
Saying, "Now that you know the great below,
We need your help on shore,
To tell your tale of being a whale and all you've seen and done.
Then wet and dry will unify,
And all the world as one will sing a whale song."
Sing a whale song.
Sing a whale song.
From the smallest ant to the tallest tree,
From the highest peak to the deepest sea.
All the world will ring in harmony
And sing a whale song!

Good Garbage

I had a turkey dinner, threw the bones away.
They hauled them to the county dump without delay.
By the following Thanksgiving they had turned to clay.
They're bio-de-, bio-de-, biodegradable garbage.

Good garbage breaks down as it goes.
That's why it smells bad to your nose.
Bad garbage grows and grows and grows.
Garbage is s'posed to decompose.

Now, Styrofoam is bad; it lasts a thousand years.
A packing peanut's born and never disappears.
So crumple up your comics when you ship your chandeliers,
'Cause comics are bio-de-, biodegradable garbage.

Good garbage breaks down as it goes.
That's why it smells bad to your nose.
Bad garbage grows and grows and grows.
Garbage is s'posed to decompose.

Every time that we buy food, we also buy the package.
Bottles, boxes, bags, and cans, they end up in the garbage.
Half of all our cash
We're spending on our trash.
For the sake of Mother Earth
Let's get our money's worth!
Only buy bio-de-, biodegradable . . .

Good garbage breaks down as it goes.
That's why it smells bad to your nose.
Bad garbage grows and grows and grows.
Garbage is s'posed to decompose.

Good garbage breaks down as it goes.
That's why it smells bad to your nose.
Bad garbage grows and grows and grows.
Garbage, garbage, garbage
Is s'posed to decompose.

Someone's Gonna Use It

When you stand at the sink, did you ever think
About the water running down the drain?
That it used to be in the deep blue sea
And before that, it was rain.
Then it turned to snow for an Eskimo
To use in a snowball fight.
Then it floated south till it reached your mouth
To help you brush your teeth tonight....

Someone's gonna use it after you.
Someone needs that water when you're through.
'Cause the water, land, and air,
These are things we've got to share.
Someone's gonna use it after you.

When you sneeze like thunder, did you ever wonder
If the air you set in motion
Might have helped to form a tropical storm
Way out in the western ocean?
Could have been blown out of a blue whale's spout
As he dove beneath the seas?
And now that air is in your care
Till you're finished with your snee—*ah—ah—ah*

Someone's gonna use it *ahchoo!*
Someone needs to breathe it when you're through.
'Cause the water, land, and air,
These are things we've got to share.
Someone's gonna use it after you.

Like a wheel the world is turning,
Forest green and sky of blue.
It will turn that way forever,
As the old is born anew.

Someone's gonna use it after you.
So leave it as you'd like it when you're through.
'Cause the water, land, and air,
These are things we've got to share.
Someone's gonna use it after you.

Someone's gonna use it after you.
So leave it as you'd like it when you're through.
'Cause the water, land, and air,
These are things we've got to share.
Someone's gonna use it after you.

This Pretty Planet

This pretty planet
Spinning through space,
You're a garden,
You're a harbor,
You're a holy place.

Golden sun going down,
Gentle blue giant
Spin us around.

All through the night,
Safe till the morning light.